Circle of Love

Mary Walters

Published by Mary Walters, 2022.

CIRCLE OF LOVE

First edition. November 22, 2022.

Copyright © 2022 Mary Walters.

ISBN: 979-8215240014

Written by Mary Walters.

Table of Contents

ONE – GETTING IN TOO DEEP

"Miss Ellis, are you busy?"

Dani Ellis looked up from the papers she was grading and regarded the young girl in front of her.

"No, Shelley. Come on in."

Dani studied the sixteen-year-old as she made her way into the classroom. Clearly something was wrong but before Dani could ask Shelley burst into tears.

Getting up quickly and making her way to the girls' side, Dani put her arm around the shaking shoulders.

After easing the student into a desk and seating herself in the one beside her, Dani asked the obvious question.

"Shelley, what's wrong?"

"Oh, Miss Ellis, my life is over!" She sobbed.

"Now, Shelley, what could be so bad to make you think your life is over?"

"Everything is wrong!" She cried some more.

Handing the distraught girl a tissue, Dani let her cry.

After giving her a few more seconds, the teacher reached out and tilted her student's chin up and pushed the long blonde hair away from her face so she could see her eyes.

"Shelley, I can't help you if you don't tell me what's wrong. You're going to have to calm down long enough to do that, okay?"

The teenager nodded through damp eyes.

"All right, now blow your nose and please stop crying for a few minutes so we can talk."

After having done as instructed and taken several deep breaths, the girl tried to explain.

"Well, you know I like Josh, right?"

Dani reflected. That would be Josh Wright. A senior to Shelley's sophomore status. Captain of the football team. Voted Most Handsome. Of course, every girl in school liked Josh.

"Right, yes, it seems I have heard that mentioned before." Dani nodded as she spoke.

"Well, he asked me to go out." Shelley started to cry again.

Dani smiled. "Shelley, why are you crying? Because Josh Wright asked you for a date? I can't see why you'd cry about that! I would think you'd be thrilled."

Shelley stopped crying long enough to look at her as if she'd grown two heads. "No, Miss Ellis. Not for a date. To go out!"

She started sobbing again.

Dani had to sit there and think about it for a moment and then she realized her mistake with the terminology.

"Oh, you mean like go steady, go together, to be boyfriend and girlfriend. Sorry, that went right over my head at first."

Dani was still processing this new development when it dawned on her. Wait, she thought, this was every girl's dream, right? Why was Shelley so upset and still crying?

"So, Shelley, this is still great news, isn't it? I mean, Josh Wright wants to date you exclusively. This should be wonderful news but you're apparently not excited at the prospect. Why not?"

"I am excited. Very much so. He gave me his class ring and I've been dying to wear it on this chain around my neck ever since he gave it to me but I'm afraid to."

Big tears rolled down Shelley's cheeks.

"I like him so much, Miss Ellis. He's such a gentleman when we're together." Shelley blushed a little. "I had heard such horrible stories from some of the older girls about how he rushed and pushed them for sex on their dates and about how crude he acted around his friends, but he doesn't act like that at all when he's with me."

Just out of curiosity, Dani asked, "How many times have you actually been together?"

Shelley got a dreamy look on her face as she described the few times she and Josh had shared lunch in the cafeteria or in his car. A couple of times, he'd taken her home from school, but she'd never invited him inside.

"Today at lunch, when he asked me to go out, I told him I wanted to but wasn't sure I was could." Shelley practically whispered the words as if they were the worst mistake of her life.

Dani just starred at her. "Shelley, are you afraid of getting hurt? Is that it?"

Shelley replied with a dreamy expression. "No, I'm not scared of him hurting me. I think we'd be great together even if we did decide to have sex. The chemistry between us is really strong and sometimes when we're making out, I don't want to stop."

Dani tried to keep her face neutral but apparently it didn't work.

"Oh, Miss Ellis, don't look so shocked." Shelley soothed her teacher.

"I'm not shocked." Dani laughed. "I'm not so old that I don't remember those feelings. You just scared me for a second when you smiled that little smile of yours."

Even though Dani laughed it off, she was a little taken aback by Shelley's attitude about the sex thing. She was not a prude but from what Shelley had just said, she and Josh had not even been on a real date, yet Shelley was considering him as her first. It seemed surprising to Dani that's all.

After they laughed for a few seconds, Shelley remembered her misery from earlier and the tears began to roll again.

"Oh, Miss Abbot, I wanted to say yes so bad, but just couldn't."

"So let me get this straight." Dani said. "You really like Josh. There's great chemistry between you. He's asked you out. Please explain to me what's standing in your way?"

"It's my dad, Miss Ellis! He'll never let me have a boyfriend." Shelley began to cry again. "I've tried to explain it to Josh but I don't think he really gets it."

Dani frowned. "Is your dad concerned because Josh is two years older or does he just think you are too young to be tied down to one person?"

"No, it's not his age. It's the fact that he's a boy. Never in a million years, Miss Ellis, will he let me have a steady boyfriend until I graduate high school as valedictorian and receive a full scholarship to Xavier which, of course, is where he went so, I have to go there, too, or..."

"Shelley, whoa! Breathe! Way too many sentences together. Remember what I've been teaching you?"

Taking a deep breath, Dani smiled at her best and brightest pupil. "Well, now I see your dilemma."

Clearly, Shelley's dad had high expectations of his daughter. He'd probably been telling her of this plan since she was a child. Shelley obviously did not want to disappoint him but the pressure from those expectations had to be tough on a sixteen-year-old.

"Shelley, even though you and I are, well, close as student and teacher, I really don't know anything about your home-life." Dani started hesitantly. "What about your mother? Can she help smooth things over with your father?" Dani asked. "You know, soften him up a little?"

"Miss Ellis, I thought you knew. My mom's dead. She died of cancer when I was ten. You weren't here then but my dad took it really hard."

"Wow." Dani said quietly. "That must have been really tough on both of you."

"Yeah. He told me later that if it hadn't been for me and his faith, he probably wouldn't have had the will to go on after she passed away."

Whew! Talk about pressure! This dad had really laid it on his kid. He'd put her in an almost impossible position; according to his plans for her, she either followed the path he laid out or she would be a failure in his eyes. Of course, if she failed him, she'd feel like a failure herself and, therefore, carry that burden forever.

Dani knew this was way of her range of expertise. She was not qualified to provide the kind of help this girl needed.

"Shelley, maybe you should talk to the school counselor about this." Dani made this suggestion because she knew it was the logical next step. However, she wasn't prepared for Shelley's response.

"No, Miss Ellis, I can't." Shelley stated very matter of fact. "Mrs. Abbott's a good counselor and is helpful with scholarships and stuff, but I couldn't talk to her about this."

"But, Shelley, she's trained to help you sort out problems like these."

"No, I couldn't possibly talk to her!" The girl stated emphatically.

"Why, Shelley? Again, I just don't understand." Dani asked quizzing. "What if I went with you? Would that help make things easier for you?"

"Thanks for the offer but there are other reasons why I can't confide in her."

"Like what?" Dani asked.

"Well, first of all, she's my Sunday school teacher and has been for a long time. Secondly, she dated my dad for a while."

"I'm sorry, Shelley, but neither of those are really very good reasons for why you won't discuss this with her." Dani stated with authority. She'd always told her students that she would not treat them as little children. She talked with them with respect and honesty.

Dani continued. "I'm sure Mrs. Abbott is enough of an adult and a professional to be able to put aside her personal feelings and help you in a time of crisis."

Shelley sat there shaking her head. "Sorry, but you're wrong, Miss Ellis. She's not like that with me at all. Even the other kids have noticed it. Since she and my father quit dating, she won't even look at me at school. She's even worse at church. In fact, I haven't gone to Sunday school in a long time. She completely ruined it for me."

Shelley continued, "Some of the kids said she's bitter because she was dumped by her first husband and then by my father so she's just mad at the world or as least at men in general. It seems as though she's mostly angry with me because I think my dad told her he couldn't date her anymore because he had to focus on taking care of me."

Dani spluttered. "Shelley, as your Language Arts teacher, I'm obviously not doing a good job because you keep stringing all these sentences together. It's just grammatically incorrect."

Shelley just laughed at her. "Oh, Miss Ellis! Not everyone can talk like you do. Especially a teenager in love!"

"I know but being in love doesn't mean you have to lose your mind and start talking like a, like a, an addled-brain, uninformed, person." Dani explained.

Shelley just looked at her with those big watery eyes and waited.

"Okay so maybe you have a reason to be somewhat addled-brained." Dani laughed.

"Now back to topic at hand which was your inability to discuss your problems with the school counselor." Dani stated. "Have you ever tried to talk to your father about what is happening between you and Mrs. Abbott?"

"No way, Miss Ellis, he'd be real upset and feel like he needed to talk with her. I don't want to cause him any more problems than he's already got. Besides, there was a time when she was my favorite all-around person but, it's funny, when she and my dad stopped seeing each other, all the kids noticed a change in her. Like she lost her joyful spirit. You know what I mean?"

"I can understand her feelings, Shelley. With this being such a small community, she was probably embarrassed." Dani commiserated with the other woman.

"Yeah, well, she's changed too much. I can't talk to her about this. Like I said, she's still there teaching the Sunday school class, but she ruined it for me. I can't even go be with my friends without feeling like I'm ruining it for them, too. She makes it too awkward." Shelley sighed deeply.

Dani studied on this for a moment before responding. As much as she sympathized with Mrs. Abbott, Dani couldn't understand why the school counselor would treat a student this way; not only at school, but away from school too.

Thinking "Counselor, heal thyself," Dani decided she'd better put this conversation to an end before she got in over her head. "Well, Shelley, I'm really glad you came by today. I hope you're feeling better now but..."

"Miss Ellis, please don't say you're not going to help me? I mean after the way you helped Abby with her problems, I was just sure you'd have some good advice for me." Shelley said in a petulant tone.

"Well, honey, Abby did come to me with a problem, but I don't really remember giving her advice."

"Well, that's not what she said. She said she was having trouble with her mom being so protective and treating her like a baby. She wouldn't even let Abby get her driver's license and she's seventeen. Anyway, Abby said that you told her that in order for her mother to see her as an adult she had to start acting more like an adult."

"That's not..."

"Abby said she went to her mom and calmly explained how she felt and what she wanted. Her mother was so surprised by Abby's mature attitude, she said she'd think about it. Abby was so excited because that was more ground than her mother had ever given. She normally just says no and that's that. End of story."

"But, Shelley, I didn't tell her to go do that. I simply tried to get her to see things from her mom's point of view."

"Well, whatever you said worked because she's happier now than she was before. So, what do you think I ought to do?"

As her student sat there expectantly waiting for a solution to her problems, Dani realized she was in big trouble. Best to put this relationship back on a different level.

"Shelley, as your teacher, I can't really tell you what to do with your personal life." Dani said as she sat back in her chair trying really hard to distance herself from the situation.

"Please, Miss Ellis. Please, I really don't have anyone else I can talk to about this. There's no one else I can ask for advice. Please just tell me what you would do if you were in my place."

"Oh, no! I can't do that, Shelley. Our situations are too different. Don't you see? In some ways, my childhood better resembles Abby's. My parents were estranged, and I never knew my father. My mother worked most of the time to pay the bills. I spent quite a bit of time by myself and grew up quicker than she would have liked. Which means sometimes I made good choices but sometimes I made bad choices that would really hurt her and, of course, it hurt me, too."

"But don't you see, Miss Ellis? At least you got to make your own choices. My dad doesn't give me any choices at all. He's got my whole life mapped out." Shelley sighs deeply. "If I lose a chance to have a relationship with Josh, I might as well give up because he's the best. I'll never love anyone as much as I love him."

Dani knew this wasn't true but when you're sixteen and in love for the first time, it felt like there would never be another love so true or anyone else to replace them in your heart. Besides this was the first time Shelley had expressed this amount of passion. Up to this point, she'd been saying she really liked him a lot and that there was great chemistry. Now it seemed more than that.

Most of the girls Shelley's age thrived on high drama but Shelley typically wasn't one of them. Dani grew apprehensive and tried to lighten the mood just to take the edge off.

"Oh, Shelley, hon. You're just starting out on the long and glorious road of being a heartbreaker. You will leave a string of broken hearts behind you." Dani attempted to laugh.

Soulfully, Shelley looked at her teacher. "Maybe so, Miss Ellis, but I think a girl only has one guy like John Wright in her lifetime."

Listening to the teenager cry as if her heart had been ripped from her chest, Dani knew she had no choice but to try and find some way to help her through this rocky time in her life.

"Okay, Shelley, I'll think about it and maybe together we can come up with a plan."

"Really? Oh, thank you, Miss Ellis, thank you! Would you please go talk to my dad?"

"I said I'd think about it, Shelley! As far as going to speak with your father, I'm not sure I'd be the best one for that. He needs to hear these things from you, not someone with no children and no qualifications as a counselor."

"I thought you'd do better on your own to break the ice initially then I could face him afterwards when he'd had some time to think it over." Shelley explained.

"I don't know, Shelley. I think anytime I go to see him, you should be with me." Dani watched as the tears began to flow again.

"No! I'd rather die than face my father with this." Shelley exclaimed dramatically.

"Certainly, it can't be that bad! Maybe you're not giving your dad enough credit. I mean, surely, he only wants the best for you."

"You don't know him, Miss Ellis! He has this way of looking into one's soul and getting his way."

"You mean he bullies and intimidates you until you forget anything but doing what he wants?"

"No, it's not like that at all. I've made him sound horrible and he's not! He just loves me and wants what's best for me, but his plan for my life is not the way I see my life playing out. He just wants too much sometimes."

"Okay, okay. I'll talk to him. But just this one time." Dani sighed. Oh, no, what had she gotten herself into?

"Great! I knew you'd help! But even if you didn't, you'd still be my favorite teacher." Shelley gave her teacher a big hug.

"Right! Now when and where will be the best time and place to catch him for a little chat." Inside Dani was berating herself, Idiot! Idiot!

Shelley was gathering her books and purse to go. Having dried her tears and blown her nose.

"Oh, he's really easy to find. He spends most of the day at our church. Oh, and watch out for Hazel."

"Church? Why in church?"

"Oh, Miss Ellis, you're so funny."

Dani just starred at her.

"Oh, you really didn't know, did you? My dad is the minister at Bethel Baptist." Shelley hurried out.

Dani called out to the retreating figure, "Who's Hazel?"

Dani slumped down in her chair. Reeling from shock at the situation she had permitted herself to be drawn into. It all made sense now. Of course, he was over-protective of his daughter. She couldn't possibly give counsel to a pastor about the rearing of his daughter. Could she? No! Absolutely not!

First of all, she had no children of her own. That would be the first thing he would say. Secondly, she had vowed years before never to set foot in church again. After her experience with church-goers, she wanted nothing more to do with pious, self-righteous fanatics.

Getting more nervous just thinking about meeting with Shelley's father, Dani shuddered thinking how her own mother would react at her interacting with church people. Miriam Ellis had a worse attitude toward them than Dani ever dreamed of possessing. Practically her entire life, Dani had listened to her mother lecture against the evils of letting herself fall into the grips of a church congregation of holy rollers who spoke with forked tongues. All least they did according to Miriam.

After she calmed down, she sat at her desk and tried to collect her thoughts. She tried to think of ways she could get out of her commitment to Shelley. However, Dani knew in her heart she would fulfil Shelley's request. After all, wasn't she the one trying to teach her students about honor, trust, honesty, and responsibility? She would talk to the pastor all right but not at church.

Since she knew Shelley had cheerleading practice on Tuesdays and Thursdays and wouldn't be apt to interrupt, she'd call the minister and request an appointment with him away from his office. She'd tell him she was Shelley's teacher and needed to discuss a concern with him. It was all true. It just wasn't a school related issue on her mind.

After having devised a plan, Dani felt better and went to the teacher's workroom right then and made the call.

TWO – SLIPPERY SLOPE

Pastor John Davies was in his office preparing his weekly sermon when the office phone rang. He had the ringer turned off but could still see the flashing light. He did his best to ignore it knowing the church secretary would answer it.

When it kept flashing going unanswered, he called out, "Hazel, can you please get that?"

Hazel Warren was a fixture at Bethel Baptist. She was 82 years old and had worked as the church secretary for nearly thirty years. Everyone knew Hazel and knew she was a character. In modern terms, some said Hazel "had no filter" as she pretty much said and did as she pleased despite how her words or actions affected others. Despite her tendency to brutally tell the truth, she was a beloved figure in the community.

Thinking she didn't hear the phone, he decided to check on her.

Upon not finding her there, he called out again, "Hazel?"

"Keep your shirt on!" the elderly woman hollered back. "Can't a gal go to the bathroom without a search party being sent out?"

"The phone is ringing." He stated.

"So, are your hands broken?" she muttered as she pushed her walker toward him.

John just stared at her and reached down to answer it.

"Bethel Baptist Church, Pastor Davies speaking, how may I assist you?"

"Yes. Pastor Davies, this is Dani Ellis. I'm Shelley's English/Language Arts teacher."

Turning his back on Hazel, he lowered his voice to keep her from hearing his reply.

"Could you hold just a moment while I get back to my desk?" he asked.

"Of course, I'm sorry if I caught you at a bad time. I can always call back later." Dani said hesitantly.

"No, no. It's not a bad time. I'll be right with you." He put the call on hold and replaced the receiver.

"Who is it?" Hazel demanded. "Is it Mrs. Abbott? Because if it is, I'll set her straight!"

"No, it's not her. It's for me and I'll take it in my office."

"If I hadn't had to go, I could have told them you weren't supposed to be disturbed and made 'em call back." She sputtered as she stumped her walker over to the desk.

"Hazel, it's okay. I've got it but thank you for your concern."

"Me, concerned? Ha! Just trying to do my job, that's all."

He closed the door as she finished the sentence and rushed over to his desk to take the call.

"Yes, Mrs. Ellis. Thanks for waiting; what can I do for you?"

"I was wondering if it would be possible for you and me to sit down and talk about Shelley. I think 30 minutes would be enough time."

"Absolutely, Mrs. Ellis. Is everything all right? Is there anything I should be concerned about?"

"No, no. Not at all, Pastor. I just need a few minutes of your time and, by the way, it's Miss Ellis or Dani, please."

"Of course, Miss Ellis. I'd like to meet as soon as possible. Could we meet today after school?"

"Yes, that would be wonderful. Maybe the local diner for a cup of coffee? My treat?" Dani queried?

John knew how the rumor mill would run wild with his meeting a teacher for a coffee date.

"That sounds nice but how about we meet at my home. It's just behind the church and I often have meetings there. We can sit out on the patio with our coffee."

"Perfect." Dani agreed. "I will see you then."

John had just disconnected when the door to his office suddenly burst open and his sister Irene charged in. Terse as usual.

John looked at her and called out, "Hazel!"

"What!? You know she doesn't listen to me, Pastor. She's not a relative of mine or she'd know better." The older woman cackled at her own joke.

Irene closed the door quickly to shut out the laughter.

"Hello, John. I'm sorry to barge in on you like this but I had to talk with you right away."

She continued on as if he were listening to every word. "I recently had the most disturbing conversation with Abigail. However, you would have been proud of me, John. I did as you suggested. I listened to her demands and instead of saying "no" immediately, I told her I'd think about it. There! Aren't you proud?"

"Irene, come on in." John knowing his sister when she was in this mood, he knew he would have to work on Sunday's sermon later.

He should be used to it by now. Everyone in this town knew his schedule. With the exception of an emergency, he used this time every week to prepare his sermon. He didn't like thinking of himself as inflexible but because of the unplanned phone call and meeting scheduled by Shelley's teacher, he was already distracted and losing a large chunk of the day. Now his own sister blatantly disregarded the rules and interrupted him. Surely God was testing him.

"Oh, dear, John. I've intruded on your sermon preparation time." Looking forlorn, Irene sniffed. "I'm so sorry. I didn't even think about the time. I just wanted to share with you. Can you forgive me?"

Smiling, he stood and walked around his desk to hug his sister. "It's wonderful seeing you so happy. Of course, I forgive you, Irene."

"Ha!" She laughed. "I knew you would. You are after all a pastor. You have to forgive everybody, right?"

John frowned at her candor then replied. "It's not always my forgiveness that is needed. I try to forgive all the time as we are instructed. However, God says when forgiveness is requested, it is received."

"Very prophetic, John, but somehow you don't sound convincing or is it convinced?"

Growing flustered with his sisters' usual directness, he asked. "Irene, please may we get to the point of you being here?"

"Oh, touched a nerve, didn't I?" She continued on quickly. "Well as I explained when I so rudely burst into your office. My daughter and I had a talk. She initiated it. She listed her requirements as she saw them. Instead of telling her no like I usually do, I asked her to give me some time to think about it."

Knowing how hard it must have been for his impulsive, impatient, and controlling sister to listen and not react, he admitted he was proud of her.

"So, what do I do now, John?"

He starred at her. He didn't want to have to make these decisions for her, but he knew she was alone and needed his brotherly guidance.

"Well, I'm assuming Abby's biggest requirement was that she be allowed to get her driver's license, right?"

Irene jumped up and started pacing.

"Yes, that and that she be allowed to get a part-time job at the mall which leaves me terrified. John, I know I can't keep her a little girl forever, but I just was not ready for her to become so independent of me."

"Irene, she's a junior in high school."

"Yes, I know. She's been harping on me to get her hardship license since she was fifteen." His sister turned anguished eyes to him. "But John, you know I can't let her do that. I just can't take that risk of losing her. She's all I have in this world."

John caught her hand as she marched past and pulled her into the chair next to him.

"Irene, we've been over this before. There's a big difference in trusting God to be in control and trying to control things all by yourself."

"I know, John, I do know. I really do know this in my head, but in my heart, I don't think I can stand losing another child."

Trying to maintain her composure, she glared at him.

"Besides, you're just as bad as I am, and you know it."

John's face took on a stunned expression. No one had talked to him like that in a long time.

"You are, John. Think about it. You're so strict with Shelley, it's ridiculous. She barely gets to go to school and back."

Gritting his teeth, he said. "I gave in on the cheerleading, didn't I?"

"Oh, yes! I'd forgotten about that. You did give in, didn't you? In fact, you were so "not controlling" with daughter that you accompanied her to the meeting on the day they got measured and fitted for uniforms. You made sure your daughter's skirt was two inches longer than anyone else's." Irene reminded him heatedly.

"Hey, wait a minute! I'd already compromised on that one because I really wanted it four inches longer." He spouted.

"Right! What a compromise! You really caved in on that issue but what about the top to the outfit?" She continued to pound on him.

"What about the top part?"

"You practically had them dressing in an extra-large t-shirt with long sleeves!"

"Well, it would have been better, definitely more practical, for those cool nights." He said trying to justify his actions.

"No, it would have been shapeless and unflattering. Those girls would have been embarrassed wearing that uniform onto the field."

"Come on, Irene! Really? Did you see their first choice? It was scandalous! Half their stomachs showing, and it had an almost nonexistent back to it. Way too much of my little girl was showing!"

"Well, I guess it worked out okay considering you tried to run the whole meeting." She said snapping at him.

He immediately snapped back. "I wouldn't have felt the need if their sponsor hadn't been running late and had been better organized."

"Whatever! I was five minutes late, John Davies, and we don't usually pass out agendas at those meetings. They're pretty informal and somehow, we've always managed to get the job done."

"Not with my daughter, you haven't." He scoffed.

"Oh, that's right. This is the first year you've consented to let Shelley tryout."

"She never mentioned it before." He lowered his voice.

She raised her voice. "She was afraid to."

"Like your daughter is afraid to discuss driving."

"My Abby isn't afraid of anything but, on that subject, I don't see Shelley with her license yet."

John turned red.

"She'll be enrolled in the parent-teach program next summer."

"Let's see, that's where you control everything and, by the way, she'll be seventeen by then. Have you discussed it with her yet?"

"No, it hasn't come up?"

"Well, it will and until then don't even talk to me about it, Brother."

"Irene, why are you here? To torture me or make me realize I'm an inept father?"

Seeing the tortured look on his face, Irene relented. "Oh, honey, I'm sorry I came down on you so hard." She says as she hugs him. "When it comes to parenting, none of us are prepared. We're all inept and, yes, we're all tormented by our fears so that's why we must trust God to help us out, right?"

John smiled at her. "Trust Him to take care of us and our children."

"Yeah, but it's so hard. So scary to let go."

They shared a quiet moment then Irene spoke.

"I just remembered there was another reason I came over."

"Oh, yeah. What was that?"

"Abigail's newfound approach to talking with me came to her through the advice of one of the high school teachers. You know the new sophomore English teacher that was hired after the year had begun?"

"Oh, yeah, I've heard Shelley mention her. Miss Ellis. She replaced old Mr. Langley."

"Yes, poor thing. Mr. Langley, that is. Died in his sleep during the second week of school."

"Yeah, that's right. He was Methodist so I really didn't know him."

Irene looked at her brother strangely. It wasn't like him to speak so nonchalantly. "John, we did know him. He taught school in this town a long time. He taught both of us, in fact. Need I remind you, Pastor, Baptist or Methodist, God values all life."

"I'm sorry, Irene. I didn't really mean it like that."

John looked at her, ashamed of himself, for having been called out and given an attitude adjustment.

"Thank you for correcting me. I realize now how it sounded."

"Well, back to what I was saying, this Miss Ellis must be well liked. I hear from Abby that "she's really cool"; "more like one of us than a teacher" and they're all going to her for advice about everything from their love lives to how to handle their parents."

John looked at her with a confident air. "Well, I'm sure Shelley hasn't consulted with her. She and I have an open relationship so she wouldn't need help talking to me. As far as her love life, there's nothing to discuss. Shelley has her priorities straight and boys are not in the plan."

Irene looked at him like he just arrived from another planet. "Oh, John." She sighed. "Is that what you really think?

"Of course, it's what I really think, Irene." John stated emphatically.

"Well, I beg to differ and, you, my friend, are in for shock. Shelley is a beautiful girl. A beautiful, normal girl. Just like her mother was I might add."

He started to say something to her, but she threw up her hand to halt his words.

"I know, I know! Elena was an angel in your eyes, and I wouldn't dare to do or say anything to tarnish that image but, John, she was also my best friend and I remember when we were sixteen all we thought about were boys."

She continued. "You might be convinced that Shelley has her "priorities in order" mimicking his deep voice, but that doesn't mean boys are not interesting to her and interested in her."

He looks at her smugly as though he knows something she doesn't.

"John, I know you're a man of great faith. It was your faith and God's strength that pulled me though when my sweet, little Katie died, and Evan left me. It was your faith with God's help that pulled us through when Elena died. Your strength and the grace of God has held this community together more than once."

"It's all God's strength, Irene. Not mine. I'm His instrument. Without Him I'm nothing."

"You're right, of course, but, honey, I just don't want to see you hurt again."

"I won't be. It's all under control."

"John, would you listen to yourself! Children as with other things in life are unpredictable. Young birds with the need to test their wings. Sometimes they fall. If you're too unrelenting, too sure of them, you'll be crushed with disappointment when they exercise poor judgment and fail. When they let you down."

"Irene, have faith, please. God will take care of us. He always has."

"Yes, He will. I have no doubt of that. But, John, remember your own teachings. Sometimes to shape and mold our character more like His own, God will allow hurtful things to happen so we can learn and grow. It's not just about the peaks; there are valleys, too."

Getting frustrating, John vents some of it on his sister. "Irene, I don't need you to teach me about valleys. Remember me? The man whose wife died a long and painful death. Who sat by her side all those long months; the surgeries, the treatments, the illness caused by the side effects, watching, and sharing the loss and heartache with my daughter? That was me, Irene. I feel as though I've had enough valleys for a lifetime already."

Holding him, hurting for her beloved brother, Irene tried to console him.

"I know, I know. I'm sorry to resurrect that painful experience for you. You did suffer as did Shelley. But that's all behind you now. Look at the good that came from all that suffering. This town now has a breast cancer clinic where people can go for help with diagnosis, counseling, and treatment. Of course, the Victorious Cancer Walk the city holds together with the school district each year in October raises a hefty donation for breast cancer research. Whereas we had nothing before Elena's diagnosis and death."

"Yeah, it's wonderful to watch the whole community come together in support of a worthy cause such as that one."

"John, back to the main subject, just don't get complacent. We still have a lot of living to do and life has a way of shaking a person up."

"Okay, okay. Whew! You've exhausted me and completely wrecked any hopes I had of getting any work done on my sermon."

"I'm sorry but it was great talking with you."

"Yeah, it was. I've got to go. I've got a meeting."

"Really? Church business?"

"Actually, no. It's with one of Shelley's teachers."

"Oh, no. Did you call a meeting because Mr. Harvey dared to give Shelley another "B" in pre-calc?"

"No." He smirked. "The meeting is with the new English teacher we were talking about earlier: Miss Ellis."

"Really? Did she say why?"

"No. I'm not exactly sure. All she said was that she needed to talk with me about Shelley. She really didn't say why."

"Hmmm. Wonder what's up?" Irene sounded thoughtful. "Want me to go with you?"

"No, no. I can handle it. I'm sure it's nothing anyway. Shelley's probably preaching in class again." He puffed proudly. "You know how opinionated she is and sometimes she gets on her soapbox to tell others about it. Miss Ellis probably wants me to restrain Shelley from running her class." He snickered.

"Maybe. Call me as soon as the meeting is over, okay? Is she coming over here or are you going to the school."

"She first suggested coffee at the diner, but I knew how that would look to everyone else, so I asked her to come here."

"Right you are. People would have you two engaged by the end of the week." She laughed. "Well, keep the shades open and stay in plain sight so as not to feed the rumor mill."

"Now you're making me paranoid." John said. "Maybe when she arrives, I'll just bring her to the office."

"Probably would be best now that you mention it. Bye, Bro!"

THREE – TAKING THE LEAP

Running late, as usual, Dani pulled up in front of the address she'd gotten out of Shelley's folder at school.

She must be out of her mind for doing this. What had she been thinking? Oh, she knew what had happened. She'd relented to Shelley's request because she really liked the girl and couldn't stand seeing her star pupil so distressed. Plus, it was her nature to want to help and please people.

Her mother had always called her a people-pleaser and told her that nothing good could ever come of it. She'd always told Dani that people were a bad investment and would let you down. They would break your heart whenever they could; at every opportunity.

Sighing, Dani looked in the mirror and tried to do something with her unruly curls to make herself appear more adult-like. Being so short, four feet eleven inches, with such a tiny frame, gave the illusion of youth immediately to most people when they first met her. She'd been treated like a child most of her life because of her size. This, of course, only fed her determination to prove to them that she was a grown, capable woman with the credentials to back it up.

Once again remembering her mother's hard-nosed teachings, Dani climbed from the car, squared her small shoulders, and walked toward the front door.

John Davies opened the door to find a tiny, elfin girl on his doorstep. Doing something he'd been trained not to do, he acted on his first impression.

"I'm sorry, honey, Shelley's not home. You'll probably catch her at school at cheerleading practice." Throwing out his wrist, he checked his watch. "Yes, she's still at practice. Do you want me to tell her you came by to see her?"

At first, Dani stood there too astonished, too shocked to respond then before she could stop it, a spark of anger just burst from within her.

"No, I'm sorry, sweetie, but I'm not here to see Shelley. It's you that I have an appointment to see."

Taken aback at the fire that leaped from her eyes and mouth, John didn't hear all the words. He wasn't accustomed to being addressed in that manner and all he could do was just stand there.

Immediately regretting her hasty actions and words, Dani tried to recover.

Sticking out her hand, Dani began again. "Mr. Davies, I'm Dani Ellis. I'm Shelley's English teacher. We had an appointment?"

Immediately contrite, he took her hand in his. Still reeling from how quickly he'd jumped to a wrong conclusion, he made another mistake. He hadn't expected an iron grip on such a tiny creature. Her hand seemed as small and childlike as the rest of her but as his big hand engulfed hers, she applied pressure and made him wince before he pulled his hand away.

"Miss Ellis, I am so sorry." He said as he attempted to rub some life back into his hand. "I'm afraid I thought you were someone else."

"It's okay, Mr. Davies. It happens all the time."

He stood there continuing to rub his hand and stare at her.

"May I come in?" she asked.

Regaining his composure, he moved quickly out of the way. "Oh, yes. Certainly. By the way, that's quite a handshake you've got there."

"Thank you." She replied. "That is courtesy of my mother, I'm afraid. Big believer in a strong handshake to convey a sense of one's character."

As she walked past him, he again noted her small stature. Being six feet two inches tall, he realized her head was barely level with his chest.

Attempting to put her at ease in his home, he led the way. "You mentioned coffee so I made some for us to enjoy while we talk. I must admit I'm rather curious about why you are here."

While he prepared a tray to take onto the patio, Dani took in her surroundings. It had a homey, welcoming feeling. Dani could easily imagine Shelley thriving in this environment. No wonder she was so well adjusted.

"You have a nice home, Mr. Davies." Dani said as she took followed him outside.

"John, please, or just Pastor. Thank you. Shelley and I have been very happy here. You should visit Bethel Baptist sometime. We've a growing congregation of over one hundred people. We have a wonderful young adult program I'm sure you would enjoy."

When she didn't respond, he continued.

"I was born here." He said as he sat the tray on the table between them. "Not in this house but in this town. We've lived in the parsonage since the year before Shelley's mother died."

Dani thanked him and reached for the cream and sugar.

"Yes, Shelley, did mention her mom had died. Cancer, wasn't it?"

Dani regretted her words as she looked up from stirring her coffee and saw the flash of pain cross his face.

"I'm sorry, Mr. Davies. That was thoughtless of me.

"No, it's okay. It was a long time ago and please call me John."

Realizing the time was nearing when she'd have to explain her reason for being there, Dani attempted more small talk.

"So, you have you always been a pastor?"

"No, when my wife and I first married, I was working construction."

"I'm not surprised. You do seem more like the rugged outdoorsman than a man sitting behind a desk all day."

John laughed at her assessment. "You know, you and my secretary have a lot in common."

"Really?" she asked. "Why is that?"

He chuckled. "Let's just say Hazel has no problem speaking her mind."

"Oh, that makes sense now." She replied.

"Why is that?" he asked.

Now she laughed. "The last thing Shelley told me was to "watch out for Hazel.""

They laughed together.

Knowing her reprieve was over and not willing to listen to him extol the virtues of the church and possibly question her spiritual status, Dani decided to jump right in.

"Mr. Davies, John, I'm sure you're curious as to why I wanted to talk with you."

"Yes, I did mention that earlier." He grinned at her.

"Yes, well...I didn't intentionally mean to be vague over the phone, but I felt it would be better to discuss things with you in person. I hope you will consider that after I've stated my situation.

"Miss Ellis, er..Dani, this is beginning to sound ominous. Have Shelley's grades begun to slip because I assure you, she knows the consequence of that. Her plans would be jeopardized if her GPA falls, and she doesn't graduate as valedictorian. She knows she must stay focused to attain the goals she's set for herself. I'll speak to her about this tonight and get it straightened out."

"John, please stop. It's not about grades. Her grades are excellent. Shelley's my brightest and best student. I'm here on a more personal note."

"Personal? How could you be personally involved with my daughter?"

"John, please calm down. She is my student and I try to take a personal interest in all my student's. The reason I'm here today is not so much of an "involvement" as I'm here at her request. She stopped by my classroom today and was distraught."

"Distraught?" He exclaimed loudly. "What do you mean? Has someone hurt her or spoken to her in such a way to upset her? If I need to go speak to the principal, I will. Dan Jones and I graduated together so I have no problem going to talk with him."

Feeling the situation was quickly escalating out of control, Dani tried to rein him in. "Please, Pastor Davies, everything's okay. No one at school has hurt Shelley. She stopped by my classroom today to ask for advice on how to approach a specific topic and talk with you about it."

That sent the Pastor reeling. "To me! I don't believe it. Why would Shelley go to a virtual stranger to ask for advice on how to talk to her father? She knows I'm always here for her to help her in any way I can."

Dani tried to explain. "Sometimes it's easier to talk to a third person, an objective third party whose opinion would be unbiased by prior knowledge of a situation."

"So, you're saying she came to you because you don't have a history with her or me and would be able to give her unclouded advice?" He sneered at her.

"Yes, that's it exactly. That and the fact that she likes and trusts me not to steer her wrong."

His eyes nearly leapt out of his head. "Steer her wrong! Are you implying I would do such a thing? Her own father? Lady, you've got to be out of your mind! Why I can think of several people she could turn to for advice that would not steer her wrong."

"Like the school counselor?" Dani asked.

"Susan Abbott? Yes, in fact, she does come to mind. She's a professional and a friend of Shelley's. I don't understand why Shelley would choose you over her. A little slip of a girl who has barely experienced life at all." He was clearly becoming overwrought. "If anything, Shelley would view you as a girlfriend not an authority figure. Susan Abbott is certainly more qualified to deal with student's problems than you."

Dani couldn't help but ask him. "You don't think your past relationship with Mrs. Abbott might not affect the direction or advice she would give to Shelley?"

"Of course not, Miss Ellis. I don't know where you come from, but, here in this community, we support one another." He blustered. "We build each other up not tear one another down. I think you should reconsider your stance about issuing advice to your students. I don't appreciate it and, although I can't speak for all parents in the community, I don't think they would consider it appropriate either."

Determined not to lose her cool, Dani took a deep breath and counted silently to ten.

"Nothing to say for yourself, Miss Ellis?" He asked goadingly.

"I've got a lot to say, Mr. Davies, but, until you're ready to listen instead of hammer from behind the pulpit, I'm not going to waste my breath."

"Preaching is what I do, Miss Ellis, so call me Pastor Davies."

Rising from the table, Dani took her untouched cup and saucer to the sink. Even though she was shaking horribly, she managed to sit them down without even a chip or spill.

Turning to him, she said. "Mr...Pastor Davies, I can't say more without betraying your daughter's trust. However, I recommend you talk with her when she comes in. She loves you very much and doesn't want to disappoint you. She also doesn't want to incur your censure like I've just been subjected to. She's trying to live up to all your expectations but inside she's struggling to become a young woman."

Almost at the front door, she turns to him again. "Please, I implore you to listen to her instead of preaching to her or you just might lose her."

"Good day, Pastor Davies."

FOUR – OUT OF THE LION'S DEN

She felt his eyes boring into her back as she left the house. However, she glanced back as she got into the car, and he was gone.

Gone back to his tidy world in his tidy home.

The man had some nerve! Of course, Dani knew from her experience with parents that they got extremely emotional and defensive when their babies were involved. But it wasn't his intense reaction as a parent that surprised her. It was his unexpected one as a man of God that surprised her. Oh, well, once again Mariam was correct. Those religious fanatics were the worst kind. Acting all pious at church in front of the pastor and their peers but behaving entirely different when not under church scrutiny.

He'd called her a slip of girl with no experience. Oh, she had experience all right and with a pastor's son no less. He'd taught her many lessons about men of God and, after he'd taken her virginity, broken her heart, he and his friends had laughed at her. She'd been so naïve.

Tears rolled down her cheeks as she tried to steer home.

What had she been thinking going to a pastor looking for compassion and understanding? Even if it had been for someone else. Poor Shelley. Dani cried even more that she'd been unable to help her student.

What was it Mariam always said? "Don't involve your heart and you can't be hurt." Yes, Momma. You were right again. People will let you down.

FIVE – OF ALL THE NERVE

John was beside himself after Dani left. No way he was calling Irene in this state. She'd charge over there, and the drama would increase tenfold.

He tried to breathe and relax but it was useless. He did the only thing left for him to do. He dropped to his knees and prayed.

"Dear Father, I handled that so badly. Please forgive me. I love my daughter so much, Lord. She's all I've got."

No, John, I'm all you've got. Lean on me.

"Yes, Father, thank you for reminding me that I'm a mere man and should look to you for understanding and wisdom. Teach me, Lord God. Show me the way to help my daughter, your child, and the congregation of your church through their tough times. I love them so much."

No more than I do.

"I don't want Shelley to get hurt. I want to protect her."

No more than I do.

"I guess I want to be too much to her. Everything to her."

Let me take that role, Child. You lead my people.

"Yes, Father. Thank you."

John was still on his knees when his daughter arrived home.

"Dad, I'm home," Shelley called exuberantly still full of youthful energy from practice.

One look at her father's face and she knew her teacher had visited.

"Shelley, honey, we've got to talk."

"Uh, sure, Dad. Can I go freshen up first?"

"Yes, that'd probably be best." He smiled gently. "I'll start supper."

He watched her bound up the stairs like she was escaping the hounds of hell. He knew Dani had been right. It was time to listen, or he'd lose her.

John waited until they'd said the blessing and begun to eat before opening the discussion.

"Miss Ellis came to see me today. She said you'd asked her to talk to me. Is that correct?"

"Yes, sir." Fork stilled, head down. "Did she tell you what we'd talked about?"

"No, honey. I'm afraid I didn't give her much of a chance."

Her head jerked up. "Dad, what did you do to her?"

"Do?" He queried. "Nothing really. I just wouldn't let her explain why she was here. I was kind of blindsided when she said it was a personal issue because I expected her to be discussing school items with me."

"But, Dad, let me explain..."

He forged on, doing exactly what he said he wasn't going to do. "I just couldn't understand why my daughter didn't come to me herself if she had problems or personal things to discuss. Why she would need to send a complete stranger instead of turning to those who love her the most." Emotion filling his voice.

Tears began to roll down the teenager's cheeks.

"Why, honey? What's so horrible that we can't talk about it without involving your teacher?"

When his daughter didn't reply but just continued to it and cry, he rose from his seat and knelt beside her chair.

"Is it something so horrible that you can't tell me?" Wrapping her in his arms, he continued.

"I love you so much, baby. Please talk to me," he pleaded.

Once the tears subsided, Shelley told him why she'd approached Dani. She leveled with him completely. Telling him the whole story including why she'd chosen not to confide in the school counselor.

"You see, don't you, Daddy. Miss Ellis was the logical choice. She's so wise for her age and she'd already proven with Abby that she could keep things in confidence. I mean, I trusted her not to tell anybody else our business and spread rumors."

"But, Shelley, why didn't you tell me about Susan? I never even guessed she was shutting you out."

"Because, Daddy, it would have only hurt you and caused dissension at church. She's been my Sunday school teacher for a long time and she's good at it. I didn't want anyone else hurt by it. Don't you see?"

Thank you, God! He thought as he held his daughter tighter.

"You are so special, Shelley. I'm very proud of you for thinking of others as you have."

Pulling away from her so he could look into her eyes, "But, next time, please just talk to me! If I seem too busy to listen, then waylay me somehow so that I stop long enough to hear you! I should never be so busy that I don't have time for you, honey."

"Now, go wash you face, and we'll talk about this Josh Wright thing."

"Oh, Daddy, do you mean it?" Shelley exclaimed with joy!

"Yes, I do." He said grinning. "But I can tell you right now, it'll seem like moving in baby steps to you. All I'm saying is we'll go slow and see how it goes. Okay?"

"Okay!" She hugged him enthusiastically, started to leave then turned back.

"I hated having to hide things from you, Dad." Shelley admitted.

John knew the best thing he could do was to remain silent and let her confess to him. He smiled gently and nodded.

"Josh and I have sat in his car during lunch more than once and he's driven me home before." She blurted out. "I felt guilty sneaking around behind your back, but I really like him. I just didn't think you'd ever allow me to date him, so I thought the only way I had a chance at seeing him was to be secretive. I'm really sorry, Daddy. I'll come straight to you from now on, okay?

Breathing a huge sigh of relief, the pastor thanked God and gave his daughter another big hug. But she wasn't done.

"Daddy, what about Miss Ellis? It sounds like you handled things badly with her. Are you going to talk with her again?"

"I did, Shelley. I really did make a mess of it. I've asked God to forgive me. I've forgiven myself. Let's just hope she's as forgiving."

"Didn't you like her, dad? She's a really great teacher and is really cool. All the kids think so."

No answer was required. She was already back up the stairs.

Thinking back on their conversation, he wasn't sure Dani would forgive him. He had acted like a complete ass. Well, he'd acted like a defensive father with a lot of arrogance thrown in the mix. He hadn't acted like a Christian, that's for sure.

She had come to his home at the request of his daughter to try and help resolve a problem that his child had felt unable to discuss with him. He'd thrown the offer back into her face primarily because of pride.

It had taken character and courage to come see him on behalf of his daughter. Those traits alone made Dani Ellis appeal to him. But there was something else about her that kept bringing her to mind. Chuckling to himself, John knew it wasn't the iron-grip handshake that he was remembering. It was the way she'd faced him and his anger; calmly.

Although he barraged her with spite, Dani did not betray his daughter's trust but continued to fight for her just the same. An indomitable spirit. One that he hoped to see working for God. That is, if his holier-than-thou attitude hadn't squelched all hopes of that. Of course, as John well knew, all things are possible with God.

SIX – SEEKING FORGIVENESS

The next day, Irene burst into his office barged past Hazel again.

"And people say I'm rude!" They heard the secretary mutter. "A lot of good it does to sit out here and try to help the pastor when everybody just ignores."

"I'm sorry, Hazel. I wasn't trying to disrespect you. I just had to see John this morning."

John was ready for her. "It's 9:09. What took you so long?" He teased his sister.

Making herself at home, she took a seat in front of his desk. "Why didn't you call me? Abby and Shelley were on the phone an hour last night. Of course, I couldn't ask Abby to tell me about the conversation. That would be breaking the precious privacy code. But I knew something exciting was going on because I kept hearing Abby giggling and squealing. So, give."

John smirked at his sister. "Irene, your bedroom is not that close to Abby's. How exactly did you hear the giggling and squealing from her room?"

"Just you don't worry about that, my dear brother. I have my ways." She scoffed at him. "I have no intention of being completely left out of my daughter's life. I remember how it was with our mother. She didn't have a clue of what I was doing half the time."

"Oh, really?" John sat forward and leaned on his elbows. "Our mother knew almost everything we did. She only let us have the illusion of secrecy. She was a master at mystery."

"No, no, no!" Irene spluttered. "You're wrong. She couldn't possibly have known. She would have said something. She would have punished us...me."

"She was a wise one that mother of ours. I see that now. This experience with Shelley has opened my eyes. Our mother knew if she hung on too tight, we'd pull and break the strings. She gave us enough slack so she could still see us and watch over us but not enough so that we actually hung ourselves."

"Really? Give me an example, please? Tell me of a time that the wise, oracle of our mother pulled me back from the breech."

"You won't like it, Irene." He sighed. "I told Mama I wouldn't tell you then, but I think it's time for you to know."

Irene braced herself. "Okay I'm ready."

"Do you remember the night you graduated from high school? Do you remember losing your virginity that night, Irene?"

Shocked to the core of her very being that her brother would broach such a sensitive subject with her, Irene jumped to her feet.

"John Davies, how dare you!"

"Well, do you remember the night?"

Easing back into the chair, Irene shifted uncomfortably. "No. It's all a blur."

"What's the last thing you do remember, Hon?"

Fidgeting in the chair, Irene says, "I remember being with some of my friends at an outdoor movie theater. Some teenage boys came over and poured us some drinks. I don't remember much after that."

"What happened after, John?" Irene asked haltingly.

"It not pretty, let's just say that. You were supposed to be in at eleven o'clock. You'd thrown a fit about the curfew, but mama had been adamant. When you didn't come home, mama made me drive her around looking for you. When we finally found you, you were in the back seat of someone's car. They were obviously taking advantage of you. I was livid and smacked as many as I could, but Mom stopped me. They were all drunk and she was only concerned about her little girl; about getting her home safe."

Irene was sobbing loudly. "Oh, God, help me." She cried holding her middle and rocking back and forth. "Oh, my Heavenly Father."

Tears were streaming down both theirs faces by now. "We got you home, into the bathroom where Mama bathed you like you were her precious baby. I know she did her best to try and prevent a pregnancy in her old-fashioned way. When she was done, she called for me and we put you to bed as if nothing had happened."

Drying his eyes, he held his sister tightly. "She told me never to mention the incident again and I haven't until today. When you woke up the next morning, it was like nothing had ever happened with Mama. She smiled and went about her business the same as always."

Irene burst into tears again. "But not me, right? I kind of remember that part. I got up and wondered why I was home in my bed, and I blamed her for not letting me stay out all night and party with my friends."

"She never said a word!" Irene balled and balled. "Oh, John, I treated her so badly."

"It's okay, Irene. By the time, she passed away, she knew how much you loved her." John consoled her.

"Yes, there is that. But all those years, I blamed her for holding me back."

"Stop! That's enough of the past." John said trying to settle her down. "We need to look to the future and our own daughters. So, let me tell you a somewhat funny story about a blind pastor." John started. After he'd finished telling her, Irene was silent for a long time. Just collecting her thoughts.

"Irene, are you okay?"

"Not really. I knew, John. I knew about Susan Abbott shunning Shelley and the change in her attitude. I should have already talked to her about it or at least talked to you about it. She was deeply hurt when you broke it off. The seed of bitterness has taken root. It's grown and obviously affected every aspect of her life. Poor Susan. How miserable she must be. How unhappy. I feel awful for her, John."

"I know exactly how you feel. I feel the same way. Although we didn't exactly have a budding romance, Susan and I shared a deep bond in our love of the Lord. I don't think I led her on but maybe she misunderstood my feelings toward her. However, as pastor, I have no choice but to ask the committee members to select a replacement. It puts me in an awkward position, but it must be done."

"Now, John, don't act rashly. Susan's Sunday school class at least keeps her in the word of God preparing a lesson each week. It gets her here surrounded in fellowship. She needs those things. Don't you think? What if by replacing her, you push her entirely away from God? Could you live with that?"

"No, you're right. I couldn't live with that. What do you suggest?"

"Let me talk with her first. I'll tell her I've notice changes and offer my love and support. Maybe she'll open up to me. In fact, let's pray about that right now. Ask God to open the window of her heart and soften it to receive forgiveness and erase the bitterness."

After they prayed, John thanked his sister for her wisdom and discernment. He went back to work on his sermon. However, he couldn't give himself fully to hearing God's words until he'd prayed again for the softening of Dani Ellis' heart toward him.

SEVEN – HEAR WITH YOUR HEART

Dani was packing her bookbag with papers to be graded. She'd tidied up her classroom glad to have another day behind her. She loved teaching and loved her students, well most of them anyway. There were a couple she'd like to shake sometimes but she liked to think they'd eventually come around and love learning as much as she loved teaching.

One of her favorite professors had once told her that the students who loved learning and liked coming to school were easy to like and easy to teach. But the others were the students who needed her the most. By reaching those students and making a difference in their lives, a teacher could feel like they changed a child's future and truly made a difference in a child's life.

Dani believed this philosophy and tried to live it every day.

Pulling the heavy bag onto her shoulder, she was about to leave when a voice came over the paging system asking her to stop by the office on her way out. Oh well, she wasn't surprised. In fact, she'd been expecting it.

Since her conversation with Pastor John Davies yesterday, she anticipated that he would contact his good friend, Dan Jones, and she'd be called in for a conference. Conference. Right! More like she'd be called onto the carpet and told the school district would not be renewing her contract. Oh, well, she thought as she locked her door. There'd be another job for her somewhere hopefully nearby.

"Have a seat, Miss Ellis," Principal Jones instructed.

"Thank you, sir."

"Miss Ellis, Dani, I'm going to get right to the point. You're a great teacher. I can already envision our student test scores on the state exams and college entrance exams improving under your tutelage. In the short time you've been here, you've been able to revitalize the students and encourage them to want to learn. That helps us all look good. Thank you for that."

Dani smiled. "You're welcome, sir. I'm just doing my job."

"Yes, you are and again, I appreciate it. However, there has been a rather serious complaint lodged against you and that's what we need to discuss today."

"Sir, I can explain."

"Please let me finish, Dani."

Dani hung her head. The good old boy network was at work here and she felt she knew what was coming.

"Dani, we're a small community. Word gets around fast. People talk. It's the nature of the beast, I'm afraid."

"Mr. Jones, I haven't done anything wrong; not one thing I'm ashamed of or anything that would tarnish the reputation of the school district."

"I'm sure that's true. But as principal, I must take every complaint seriously and answer to our school board."

"Dani, it was reported that yesterday a student came to you as a friend and asked you to intervene with a parent on that student's behalf. Is that true?"

"Yes, sir, but I don't see how any rules were broken."

"Did you call that parent and ask to have coffee with them?"

"Yes, sir, I did, but it was going to be on my own time after school off campus."

"Did you end up meeting that parent at his home to discuss something other than your student's classroom behavior, progress, or work?"

"Yes, sir, but I still don't see that there were any rules violations."

"The rules violation was that you took a personal family situation and attempted to mediate on your own without professional advice or attention being brought to light on the situation. What you did, albeit in an honest attempt to help, could place yourself and this school district at great risk for a potential lawsuit."

"What? He's threatening to sue the district over nothing. I don't believe it. He's an even bigger hypocrite than he appeared yesterday!"

"I don't believe he'll go through with it either, but I would be remiss in my administrative duties if I did not warn you of the danger of taking such actions as you did yesterday. Look, Dani, you're young. You wanted to help one of your students. Anyone can see that you need to be more careful and less impulsive. Understood?"

"Yes, sir. I understand perfectly."

As she exited the principal's office, Dani was too upset to see Susan Abbott standing just inside her office door listening to their entire conversation.

Relieved that it was Friday, and the football team had a bye, therefore, she had no afterschool duty to perform, Dani was packing to drive down and see her mother when there was a knock on her door.

Her apartment though small was neat as a pin and sparsely but tastefully decorated. She wasn't accustomed having visitors and had no idea who was at the door, but she still looked around to be sure things were in order before she opened the door.

She was just preparing to look through the peephole when the visitor knocked again. It was John Davies! She thought about not opening it at all but then she heard Shelley's voice.

Opening the door, Dani smiled a welcoming to Shelley before glancing at her father.

"Pastor Davies," she said and nodded toward him.

Shelley walked into the apartment, confident in her youth that she was welcome, but her father held back.

"Dani, please may I come in? I've got a few things to say to you."

"I really don't think it's a good idea, Pastor. I wouldn't want a lawsuit on my hands."

He looked at her quizzingly.

"Oh, what the heck! We have a chaperone so come on in," Dani pushed the door wide open.

John made the tiny apartment feel even smaller, but Dani refused to be intimidated by him.

Shelley, oblivious to the undercurrents, charged Dani and took her by the hands to lead her toward the sofa.

"Miss Ellis, guess what? Dad's going to let me go on a date with Josh! Isn't that great? Oh, he says we have to move slowly but I feel like it's a great leap for him to allow this and I only have you to thank!"

Being on the receiving end of Shelley's exuberant hug elated Dani but she made sure she didn't respond inappropriately.

"I'm glad you and your dad were able to work toward a compromise. You didn't need me." Dani smiled and said as she placed her hand over Shelley's.

"Well, yes, but you broke the ice for me and made it easier for dad and me to talk. Come on, Miss Ellis, take some credit!" Shelley was unrelenting.

"Did you know, Dad, that Miss Ellis advised me first to go talk to you, but I was too scared. Then she tried to get me to see Mrs. Abbott but I couldn't do that either so after I cried and cried and begged, she said she'd talk to you. That's what I call a true role model." Shelley looked at Dani. "I know, I know, too many sentences run together!"

They all laughed.

"Yes, Shelley." Pastor Davies acknowledged. "You're right. She's a true role model."

The two adults stared at each other both lost in their own private torments. When Shelley asked if she could wander around and see the rest of the apartment, Dani quickly agreed.

"Sure, although that'll only take a couple of minutes or less." She laughed.

John took Shelley's place on the sofa and reached for Dani's hand which she reluctantly allowed him to hold.

"Dani, I am so sorry for what I said to you and the way I acted. Please forgive me."

She yanked her hand from his.

"You, sir, are a real hypocrite! I can't believe you come in here today talking forgiveness after what you've done!"

John looks at her completely baffled.

"Dani, I know I was hard on you but after I thought about your intentions, where your heart was, I felt awful."

"Well, you should feel awful. But don't worry I'm submitting my resignation. I won't be here next year so don't even think about filing a lawsuit."

"Lawsuit? That the second time you've said that. What's going on?"

"Resignation?" Shelley rushed in. "Miss Ellis, you're leaving. Why?" She questioned as she threw herself at Dani.

"Please don't leave, Miss Ellis. I love you. If it's something I've done. I'm sorry."

Patting the younger girl on the back, Dani tried to soothe her. "No, baby. It's nothing you've done. Don't ever think that. It's me. I messed up and I've got to find another job."

Father and daughter started talking at once. They were so loud, Dani almost didn't her the phone.

"Hello. When? Any idea how much time she has? I'm already packed so I'm leaving now. I should be there in about forty-five minutes."

She hung up the phone and looked at her visitors.

"I have to go." Dani said clearly shaken but trying to maintain a tight hold on her emotions. "That was the hospital. My mother's not expected to live through the night."

John and Shelley both rushed to her aid. "Dani, let us help you. We'll go with you."

She closed her suitcase, grabbed her purse, and herded them out the door.

"No, I don't think so, Pastor. It might cause too much talk among your people. Besides my mother hates churchy people."

Dani locked her front door and headed to her car leaving them standing there.

"At least tell us where you'll be." He called out as she was climbing into her car.

Dani drove away and didn't look back.

EIGHT – RECEIVING LOVE AND SUPPORT

"Thank you, Dr.," Dani said as the physician left the room.

Walking to her mother's bedside, Dani picked up the lifeless, blue-veined hand.

"Did you hear that, Mom? You're getting better. The doctor said it was just a small stroke and that you might recover fully. There's that chance, Mom. Please fight."

Exhausted, Dani gently laid down her mother's hand and eased herself into the chair next to the bed.

The chair had served as her bed for the last three nights. The hospital had offered to wheel a cot into the room, but Dani had declined, willing her mother to get better soon. By stubbornly refusing a bed as a sign of settling in for a long-term illness, she was indicating to herself and all others that she was not giving in to her mother's illness and was sure her mother was going to recover quickly.

On Sunday, Dani knew she wasn't going to be able to leave her mother side. She called Dan Jones and explained the situation. He told her to stay in touch and they would make arrangements for a substitute teacher for her classes. All Dani needed to do was email him the lesson plans which she did immediately.

Principal Jones also asked the name of the hospital where her mother was staying. Dani had hesitated but had given him the information. After all, he was her boss. He needed to know where to reach her, right?

The next day a lovely blooming plant arrived. It was from her coworkers wishing her mother a speedy recovery.

Dani was admiring the plant as she gathered a blanket around her shoulders and tried to grab a short nap before the nurses came in to check on her mother again.

She was awakened by a light touch on her arm.

Surprisingly, she opened her eyes to see John Davies smiling down at her.

"Hello, Dani. How's she doing"?

"Good, I guess. The doctors say it's looking good." Still befuddled from sleep, Dani tried to comprehend what was happening.

"What are you doing here? How'd you know where to find me? I don't understand why you're here?"

Before he could answer, the on-duty nurse came in to take her mother's vital signs.

Seeing this as his chance, John motioned for Dani to join him in the hall.

"I'll answer all your questions in a minute but first, please let me apologize for the way I acted the other day when you came by to talk to me about Shelley. Can you forgive me?"

Looking up into his eyes, Dani believed his apology was sincere, but she wasn't ready to give in yet.

"Pastor Davies, I accept your apology but I'm not quite ready to forgive and forget."

His face lit up the room. "Thank you, Dani. You won't regret it."

Did he not hear her? Did the words come out of her mouth wrong? She'd said she didn't forgive him. Why was he smiling?

"I don't understand," she mumbled more to herself than to him.

"No, but hopefully you soon will."

Without her realizing it, he'd walked her down to the waiting area where Shelley and Abby were watching for them.

"Miss Ellis!" Shelley rushed over to her. "How's your mother? You look so tired. Are you okay? Dad said we could come with him to see you but only if we promised not to wear you out."

Dani smiled at her precious students. "You guys wear me out just listening to you and trying to keep up." She laughed.

Seeing the girls' troubled expression made Dani realize how harsh her words might have sounded.

"Hey, lighten up! I was teasing! Of course, I'm glad to see you both! You have made my day. I've been missing my students, so this is indeed a treat!"

Abby almost as high-spirited as Shelley, "Oh, Miss Ellis, we're missed you at school. Even though I'm not in your class, I have to listen to the sophomores complain about the sub."

She grinned at Shelley who picked up from there. "Abby and I went in and read the lesson plans before the sub got there. She was with me for moral support. He didn't follow your instructions at all."

Dani was laughing at the girls take charge attitude. "What did the sub make you do?"

"A fate worse than death, Miss Ellis. He made us read the next Chapter in our Language and Composition book and then spend half an hour conjugating verbs and diagraming sentences."

"Oooh!" Dani exclaimed appropriately. "That is horrible! Torturous!"

"Girls, give her room to breathe." A female voice said from behind them.

Dani turned to see the source.

"Miss Ellis, I'm Irene Smith, Abby's mom."

"Oh, Mrs. Smith, so nice to meet you."

"Yes, it's good to finally meet you too. Shelley and Abby have talked so much about you." Eyeing her up and down, Irene grinned! "Although somehow they made you seem much taller."

Laughing, Dani replied. "I know Abby and Shelley are cousins so you must be Pastor Davies sister."

"Yes," Irene agreed. "John's my big brother." The pride obvious in her voice.

Taking Dani's small hand in hers, Irene led Dani to some nearby chairs.

"How's your mother, Dani?"

Taking a deep breath, Dani explained. "She's suffered a stroke, but the doctors are optimistic that she'll recover."

"Any paralysis?"

"Possibly. They won't know for sure for a while yet."

Irene patted her hand and released it. "We've already added her to our prayer chain which mean people are praying for her and for you around the clock."

At a loss for words, Dani smiled and nodded her thanks.

"I better get back," Dani rose to leave uncomfortable with the turn of the conversation.

Trying to detain her a little longer, John spoke up quickly.

"I told the girls we'd walk down to the cafeteria and eat a bite while we were here. I know they'd love it if you'd go, too."

Cutting him a glance making him aware that told him she knew exactly how underhanded he was to use the girls, Dani agreed to go.

Dani, however, enjoyed herself immensely. Listening to the girls talk. Catching her up on all the latest happenings at school. It was also a treat to watch the girls interact with their parents. Their obvious love and respect for one another did not surprise her. What impressed Dani the most was that Irene and John both seemed to maintain the balance between friend and authority figure. She and her mother had never been that close.

Oh, she'd respected her mother and recognized her as an authority figure, but she'd never enjoyed talking to Mariam. She never would have shared her true feelings and thoughts with her.

When Mariam had found out she was dating the pastor's son behind her back, she'd railed for days. Hadn't she learned anything? Didn't she know all men especially religious men were liars and two-faced? But instead of heeding her mother's words, she'd run straight into his arms and disaster.

After the breakup, Mariam saw Dani's broken heart and broken spirit in her eyes. Instead of holding her while she cried, Mariam guarded her like a jailer until she could see the evidence that Dani was not pregnant. Once this became clear, Mariam had sat Dani down at the kitchen table and lectured regarding pre-marital sex. Oh, not because it was against God's plan but because Mariam did not want her name sullied among the community any more than it already had been. She even offered to help Dani get birth control pills in case she was seduced again. But Dani refused. There'd be no next time for her.

Dani knew better than to ask about the scandal that surrounded Mariam's youth. Her mother staunchly refused to discuss it. Instead, she kept it inside holding it close where it had colored her entire life and her daughter's.

Dani loved her mother and knew she'd done her best. However, watching her students talk with their parents made her realize what she'd missed. Maybe one day if she ever had children, she could have this type of closeness with them.

Catching her daydreaming, she realized they were staring at her.

"I'm sorry. I must have wandered off. Were you waiting for me to answer a question?"

"No, Honey." Irene answered. "We were just discussing the arrangements for this coming week."

"Arrangements?" Dani asked.

"Why, yes, dear?" Irene explained. "Who will be staying here with you or staying with your mother if you need a break. Those arrangements." She smiled at Dani patiently.

Tugging her hand away, Dani rose. "That's awfully sweet of you but I don't need anyone to stay. I'm sure Mother will start to recover soon, and I can manage just fine on my own."

"Yes, honey, but even if she does, there could be weeks of therapy and follow-up visits. You'll need help with the driving and someone to sit with her."

Dani looked at them blankly.

Finally, John spoke up. "I don't know what kind of insurance she has, but she may even need full-time care and you will need help. We would like to do that, Dani." His eyes imploring her. "Help you, that is. There are plenty of people in our congregation even the youth that would be more than willing to help you."

Dani sunk back into a chair, suddenly feeling overwhelmed at the prospect of taking her mother home to her tiny apartment and providing her with round the clock care.

"But the doctor said she might fully recover." She whispered.

Kneeling and putting his arm around her tiny shoulders, John could feel them shaking. At that moment, he realized how deeply he cared for this woman. It was as if God had spoken to him and told him how important Dani Ellis was going to become in his life.

Afraid the intensity of his feelings would scare her; John loosened his hold on her.

"You're right, Dani, she might fully recover, and we'll all be praying for that very thing. But you can also see how important you've become to us."

Dani looked around at the hopeful, anxious faces.

John continued. "We want to help you, Dani. Please let us help you and your mother."

Dani bit her lip to restrain the tears that threatened.

She nodded her assent as they gathered her in a group hug.

Mariam would have a fit when she found herself surrounded by the Bethel Baptist volunteers.

Dani knew she'd probably regret getting involved with these church-goers but, at the moment, she was just too weak to try to fight with them. And, Dani, had to admit, John's arm around her supporting her, now and earlier, giving her his strength, was a great feeling. A feeling of loving, almost of belonging, that she hadn't experienced in a long, long time, if ever.

Mariam had indeed regained consciousness and although there was a slight paralysis on her left side, Dani could tell it would only be a matter of time before her mother returned to her usual feisty self.

Over the next few weeks, while they watched Mariam's recovery take a miraculous turn for the better, Dani couldn't help but be convinced it had something to do with the prayers being sent Heavenward each day. She didn't really join in but she sometimes she felt a pull at her heartstrings to give thanks to the one they prayed to.

At first, Mariam didn't say much about the volunteers in and out of her room. It was almost as if she thought they were part of the hospital staff.

The first-time Pastor Davies visited her mother's hospital room and introduced himself, Dani could tell Mariam didn't like it. But as his visits became almost daily routine and he never tried to preach to her, Mariam tolerated his presence and that of his family.

When he wasn't there, Mariam quizzed her daughter as to the role he played in her life. Dani always managed to deflect her mother's queries without really answering because she didn't want Mariam to know how important John was becoming to her.

However, one night as he was leaving, he completely surprised Dani, by leaning down and brushing his lips across hers. Dani realized it was more than friendship between them. The knowledge elated and scared her at the same time.

Dani was hoping her mother would let it go unnoticed but wasn't really surprised when she didn't.

"What is it with you and church men? Can't you find a real, down-to-earth, honest man to give yourself to? You know what will happen. It's happened before. After he realizes you're not lily-white and all sanctimonious like he expects, he'll leave you and you'll be heartbroken. Again!"

As the blood pressure and heart monitors went crazy, a nurse came rushing in.

"Mrs. Ellis, you've got to remain calm, or you'll break all these machines by making them work that hard."

Dani smiled at the nurse's attempt to lighten the mood. Mariam, however, was not so easily assuaged.

"I don't care about your machines or staying calm for that matter. My daughter's getting ready to lose her heart to that "preacher" and I can't just lay here and do or say nothing!"

"Now, now, honey, it can't be that bad." The nurse patted her hand as she was tried again to calm her. "After all, to be a preacher is a fine calling. She could do worse." The nurse had no idea what she was saying or the effect it would have on her patient.

"Calling?" Mariam practically screeched. "Is that what it is? When a man uses his godliness to seduce a young woman and then leaves her pregnant. When because of his selfishness and lustfulness, he lets her become the object of pity and scorn? Ridiculed and maligned by those same very holy people who professed to be God's children?"

Dani had never heard her mother speak like this and knew without a doubt she was hearing her mother's story. She understood for the first time why her mother was so bitter.

"Oh, no, young lady, I'm not letting my daughter fall into that trap. Not while I still breathe."

Exhausted by her tirade and by the sedative given to her by the nurse, Miriam slipped into a troubled sleep as was indicated by the erratic numbers showing on the machines.

Still in shock from her mother's revelation, Dani jumped when a hand touched her shoulder.

She looked up to see John beside her once again.

She jumped up and threw her arms around him sobbing into his shirt. No longer able to maintain the façade of a cool, collected schoolteacher.

When she pulled back, she asked him. "Did you hear what she said?"

Stroking his hand down her heard, he answered. "Yes, honey. I heard it all. I'm sorry. I was waiting for the elevator when I saw the nurse run toward Mariam's room. I hurried back in case you needed me."

"I'm so glad you're here. Oh, John, she's always been so miserable. Her whole life she's been bitter. Now I finally understand why. It all makes sense. My father seduced her and left her carrying me. She must have suffered so."

Dani could hardly talk through her tears. "I couldn't understand her aversion to church and church people, but I do now."

"We're not all like that, Dani. We're not perfect or superhuman. We make mistakes as you've seen." He looked deep into her eyes. "But, Dani, I would never intentionally hurt you like that."

"I know that John, but thank you for saying it."

"Can I pray for her, Dani? Right here? Right Now?" He asked. "Will you pray with me?"

Dani stammered. "I..I really don't know how. I mean I've listened to you and your family pray and it sounds so easy, like talking, but I'm not sure I can do it."

John took her hand on one side and her mother's hand on his other side.

"Sure, you can," he smiled. "It'll be my great pleasure to teach you."

As they bowed their heads, John asked for God to please lift the burden of bitterness and unforgiveness from Mariam's heart, to help her to see that not all His people were hypocrites and to give him the opportunity to visit with Mariam before it was too late."

As they walked hand in hand to the elevator, Dani worked up the courage to ask him a question that had been bothering her for weeks.

"John, there's something I need to know. After our first meeting, when I came to your house, why did you call Dan Jones and complain about me?"

He looked dumfounded.

"I honestly don't know what you're talking about, Dani. I never spoke with your boss about you." He confessed.

Now it was Dani's turn to look at a loss.

John asked her. "Does this have anything to do with the lawsuit you mentioned or your talk of resigning?"

"Well yes, actually, it has to do with both of those things." She admitted

"What exactly did he say, Dani? Did he say I'd complained?"

Thinking back, Dani remembered. "No, he never even mentioned your name. He said "he" when talking about the person who had complained, and I thought it was you. He also said that a complaint had been lodged against me for going to your home for personal reasons."

Looking at John in shock, she was contrite.

"Oh, John, I'm sorry! I assumed the worst about you from the start."

"Dani, from what I heard you mother say earlier, I'm not surprised by that." He brushed the hair back over her ear.

"But John, if it wasn't you then who was it?"

"I don't know, honey, but I'm going to find out first thing tomorrow."

NINE – SETTLING THE MATTER

The following day after John had gotten off the phone with the high school principal, he called Irene.

Getting right to the point, he asked.

"Did you ever get a chance to talk with Susan Abbott?"

"Well, yes, John, I did. She was openly bitter toward you and Dani Ellis."

"Why, Irene? I don't understand."

"Honey, you're a great pastor, but a little blind to some of the more personal side of relationships."

"That's not true. I'm very personable. I try to listen to each individual member of the congregation and help them with their personal and spiritual needs."

"And you do that very well, darling, it's just that you are so busy trying to be all things to all people you forget yourself."

"Please explain, sister dear."

"John, how many dates did you have with Susan Abbott?"

"First of all, we never dated. I asked her to accompany me to a couple of church events and once she volunteered to host a dinner at the parsonage for a visiting pastor and his family."

"To Susan Abbot those were dates, John. You were there as a couple! For goodness sakes, John, she was in love with you. She was already having visions of being your wife, a pastor's wife, and Shelley's new mother. To you, it was friendship. To her, it was more than that."

Flashbacks of the conversation between Dani and Mariam went through his mind.

Good grief! Was he really as callous as that? Using Susan Abbott's eagerness to please meanwhile leading her to believe they were more than friends? Why he'd never even kissed HER and he told Irene just that.

"It doesn't matter, John. She never realized you didn't share her feelings until you gave her your version of the break-up speech which she said was a very sweet way of saying I won't be needing your services anymore."

John gasped. "No, I never meant it that way!"

"I know, but she was deeply hurt which turned into anger. She kept teaching Sunday school, but she didn't realize how much of her feelings were spilling out onto Shelley and her class until I mentioned the kid's comments about her changing at church and school."

John sat there with his hands together as a steeple against his lips, tapping them and Irene could tell he was deep in thought.

"You never really noticed, John? It never occurred to you what was happening?"

He exhaled. "On some level, I had to have known. I guess at first, I must have just disregarded her feelings completely. Later, I ignored her, so I didn't see how she was acting. I'll need to talk with her and seek her forgiveness."

"Yes, you will. Not just for her sake but for your own. This whole situation has made me take a personal inventory of my own life and ask God to show me anyone that I need to search out to make amends."

"One thing, Irene, before you go. Did Susan mention to you that she'd complained to Dan about Dani's unprofessional behavior?"

"No, she failed mention it."

"Yes, well, he left Dani with the impression that due to her unprofessional behavior, the school district was left open to a lawsuit. Of course, she jumped to the conclusion that I had complained to him and was threatening to sue. She was prepared to resign."

"Oh, no, John. That would be a horrible mistake. According to all reports, she's a great teacher."

"I know that's why I contacted our friend the principal this morning to straighten this mess out. I told him I had already assured Dani that I was not the culprit who had called to complain about her. When I asked him point blank, however, he wouldn't tell me who it was. I made sure he understands how much we need Dani here."

"We need her here, John, or you need her here?" Irene asked smirking.

"What do you mean?"

"Does she understand how much she means to you and how much you need her?"

At first John started to deny his feelings but knew he couldn't any longer.

"No, I don't think she does. I don't think even I knew until just now."

"Don't wait too long to tell her, my sweet brother."

TEN – WHAT IT ALL MEANS

A week later, Dani was happy to be bringing her mother home from the hospital. Mariam was going to be staying with her daughter for a while until she could fend for herself completely. She was recovering nicely but Dani wasn't willing to let her go home alone just yet.

Once Dani had called to let Irene know that they were home and settled, there had been a constant stream of people in and out of Dani's small apartment bringing food and good wishes.

At first, Mariam remained sullen but, after a couple of women her age with similar problems stopped in to visit, Mariam became more animated. It was wonderful to see her mother chatting. For as long as she could remember, Dani had never known her mother to have friends. She'd never even hardly mentioned her co-workers to Dani. She just always seemed so lonely, so solitary in her misery. That misery had been her primary companion for many, many years.

Dani knew the day was coming when she and her mother would have to discuss the past. It had haunted them both long enough and it was time to let it go. She only hoped her mother would be able to do so after holding it close for so long.

She didn't know if it was because of her near-death experience or the new friendships she'd developed, but Dani was very surprised when her mother agreed to attend church services with her.

With her mother in a wheelchair, they entered the church and stayed toward the back.

Neither Dani nor her mother joined in the singing but when John stood to deliver the message both women gave him their full attention.

"Good morning, friends. It good to see everyone here today."

"I come before you today not to preach but to do something entirely different. I need to ask for your forgiveness."

Gasps could be heard from the audience.

He continued. "Not for committing some horrible sin as you might first think. Although sin is sin. What I've done is commit the sin of prideful thinking. I need to ask your forgiveness for that and for my arrogance, but most of all, for sending some of you away from God instead of helping you draw closer to Him."

"I've always believed that if a person, a professed, Christian person, says or does anything that draws another person away from God then it's one of the most heinous sins. I've done that, friends. Through blindness and ignorance of others, their feelings, and their pain, I've caused some of you to pull away from God."

"This is terrible because it has such a trickle-down effect. One person becomes angry toward another, the angry person then goes on to be hurtful to someone else and so on and on it goes. But it must stop, friends. We cannot profess in church to be Christians, followers of a loving God and then go out of here and live another way. God knows your heart. In those secret places where you're clinging to anger, bitterness, jealousy, greed, lust. He knows."

"I ask you to please not leave here today without relinquishing your hold on those feelings. Please make peace with those individuals and hurtful emotions that stand as a wall between you and God. By clinging to those feelings, you do hurt others, but you mostly hurt yourself."

"Lastly, anyone present today who I have hurt or ignored in anyway, please find it in your hearts to forgive me. I can't stand the thought of causing anyone pain or making them have emotional barriers between themselves and God. Please today let's pull these barriers down."

"I'm sorry if I've hurt any of you. Please let's start fresh today."

"Anyone who would like to come to the altar and lay your burdens there to leave behind forever, please do so. Imagine the feeling of lightheartedness and joy you will experience when those burdens are cast upon God's altar."

John left the pulpit and went to stand in front of the altar. Susan Abbott was the first to meet him there. Tears were streaming down her face as she unburdened herself to him. As they talked, Dani watched as many others came forward and knelt there around them to pray. Irene, Shelley, and Abby were among those who were kneeling.

Dani felt her mother becoming more and more agitated in her chair.

"Mom, are you okay?" She whispered. "Is it your heart?"

"Yes, baby. It's my heart but not like you mean. Help me get my chair into the aisle. I've got to go talk to that preacher-man of yours."

"Do you need my help?" Dani asked.

"No, Dani. This is something I've got to do by myself."

Watching her mother slowly make her way up the aisle, Dani smiled lovingly with tears running down her face. It filled her with joy seeing her mother take John's hand as he dropped to a knee to greet her. Yes, she'd felt like walking the aisle herself to him and to God. Somehow, Dani knew there'd be another day for her to go. That John and his family would be there to welcome her to the fold. As she watched them pray together, a peace filled her like none she'd ever experienced. Dani wasn't surprised when the two most important people on earth turned to her and beckoned her to them. She grinned and practically ran to them. She dropped to her knees and wrapped them both in her embrace as they did the same.

Dani pulled back to look into her mother's face and was amazed! Her mother was smiling and crying at the same time, but to Dani, her mother was glowing, radiant in a way that she'd never seen before. Dani could tell Mariam was free from the ugliness and bitterness which had consumed her the majority of her time on earth.

As she turned to John, who was also crying, Dani knew a peace and happiness like she'd never experienced. Shelley joined them and Dani felt complete.

Behind them, they heard a grumpy female voice say, "Can anybody get in on this, or is this a closed meeting. Move over and let me in."

They burst into laughter and wrapped their arms around Hazel, pulling her into the circle of love.

THE END